THE MIST MONSTER

KIRSTI BEAUTYMAN

KITCHEN

PARSLEY

Penny wasn't sure about the new house,
but Dad said it was a brilliant adventure.
"A great explorer like you?" said Dad.
"You'll have a grand time!"

There was just one thing missing.
"I need to find Mum's old explorer hat," said Penny.
"Then I'll be ready for anything."

Dad rummaged in a box.
"Woo-hoo! One explorer hat!
Come and get it!"

But Peanut the dog
got there first.

"Hey! Come back!" cried Penny.
"I need that hat!"

And she dashed
out after him.

When Penny got outside,
Peanut had disappeared.
She was all alone in a strange
white world. Then a voice in
the mist rumbled . . .

Penny found herself looking up into two huge yellow eyes.
It was a sort of monster. "Who are you?" she said.
"I'm not sure," said the monster. "I think
I might be made of mist."

He didn't have a name, so Penny decided to call him Morris.

Penny told Morris all about Peanut
and her missing explorer hat.
"That's terrible!" he growled. "I bet
I can find that naughty dog.
Follow me!"

But they'd only gone
two steps when . . .

. . . they landed in a pond.

"Oops! Sorry! Wrong way!" said Morris.

"Perhaps we should ask that monster over there?"
Penny peered into the mist.

THAT'S NOT
A MONSTER!
THAT'S MY
DOG!

She leapt across the lilypads.
"Come on, Morris!"

But Peanut was too
quick for them.

"Look!" said Penny.
"He's left tracks in the sand."
A trail of perfect paw prints led
out of the pond and into
the mist.

They followed the tracks for hours.

Sometimes they thought
they saw Peanut.

Sometimes
they heard him
barking.

Morris found some huge
blackberries and they ate
them under a tree.

"I can see your
blackberry in your tummy,"
laughed Penny.

Then Penny told Morris all about the new house,
and how it was going to be a grand adventure.
"I really do need my explorer hat, though," she said sadly.
"It must be a very special hat," said Morris.

"It is," said Penny. "It was my mum's.
She was a brilliant explorer."
Then suddenly they heard . . .

"Follow that dog!"
shouted Penny.

"Follow that hat!"
cried Morris. "We'll get
there faster if we roll!"

"Where's he gone now?" huffed Penny. She climbed a tree to get a better look. "I wish I could climb," said Morris, sadly. "Can't you just float up?" asked Penny.

"Oh! What a good idea!" he said, and he drifted up like a cloud.

"Look!" said Penny.
"The mist is clearing!"
"Oh . . . so it is,"
said Morris.

He sounded a little bit sad.

They could see the house now,
and there was Dad – with Peanut!

"Hulloooo!" called Dad. "Is there
an explorer out there who's missing a hat?"
"Yes! Me!" shouted Penny, and she
leapt down from the tree.

"Bye-bye, Morris! Thanks for playing."
She tried to give him a hug, but it's not
easy hugging mist. "See you tomorrow!"
"I hope so," said Morris, quietly.

That night, in her new bedroom,
Penny had the most wonderful
dreams — and they were all
about Morris.

Next morning, she grabbed
her explorer hat

and dashed
outside.

But Morris was
nowhere to be seen.

"Where's all the mist gone?" she asked her dad.
"There's no mist today!" said Dad, cheerfully. "It's a beautiful sunny day!"

Penny ran down the garden and burst into tears.
She'd found her hat – but lost Morris.
"Who am I going to explore
with now?" she said.

Then a voice said: "You can explore with me, if you like."

Penny found herself looking up into two big brown eyes.
They belonged to a boy called Archie, who lived next door.
Archie was going to be an astronaut, but he didn't
mind exploring on land, too.

The two of them had
many adventures,
in the rain . . .

in the sunshine . . .

and even in
the snow.

But the misty days . . .

. . . were the best of all!

For friends, family and Picture Hooks.
Thank you all for your time, advice, input and support.
It means more to me than I can put into words.

First published in the UK in 2019 by Alison Green Books
An imprint of Scholastic Children's Books
Euston House, 24 Eversholt Street London NW1 1DB
A division of Scholastic Ltd

www.scholastic.co.uk

London – New York – Toronto – Sydney – Auckland
Mexico City – New Delhi – Hong Kong

Designed by Zoë Tucker
Text and illustrations copyright © 2019 Kirsti Beautyman

HB ISBN: 978 1 407188 87 4
PB ISBN: 978 1 407188 88 1

The moral rights of Kirsti Beautyman have been asserted.
Papers used by Scholastic Children's Books are made
from wood grown in sustainable forests.